DER

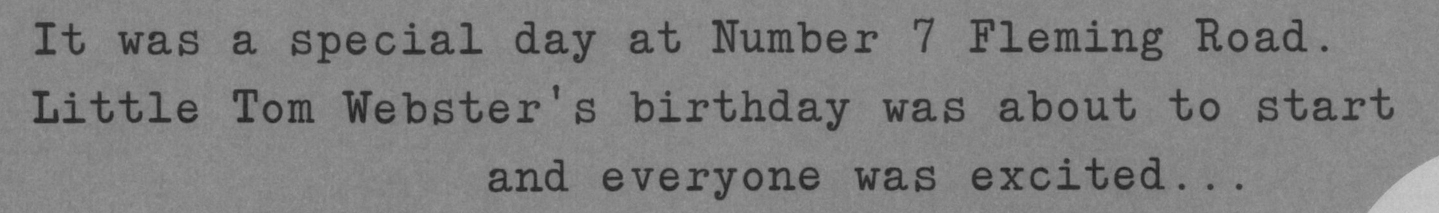

It was a special day at Number 7 Fleming Road. Little Tom Webster's birthday was about to start and everyone was excited...

...especially Spyder, the world's smallest secret agent who lived in the loft. She loved birthdays.

In her penthouse flat
Spyder had just put her feet up
(which takes quite a while when you've got eight legs).

Suddenly her spy phone rang...

It was **Headquarters**, with an urgent message.

Hello, 008.
This naughty fellow has just
entered your airspace.
If he reaches the kitchen,
Tom's precious birthday cake
could be ruined.

MISS
MONEY SPIDER

Spyder leapt
into action.

On my way, Boss. You know
I never like to miss a party!

CODE NAME: BLUEBOTTLE

TOP SECRET

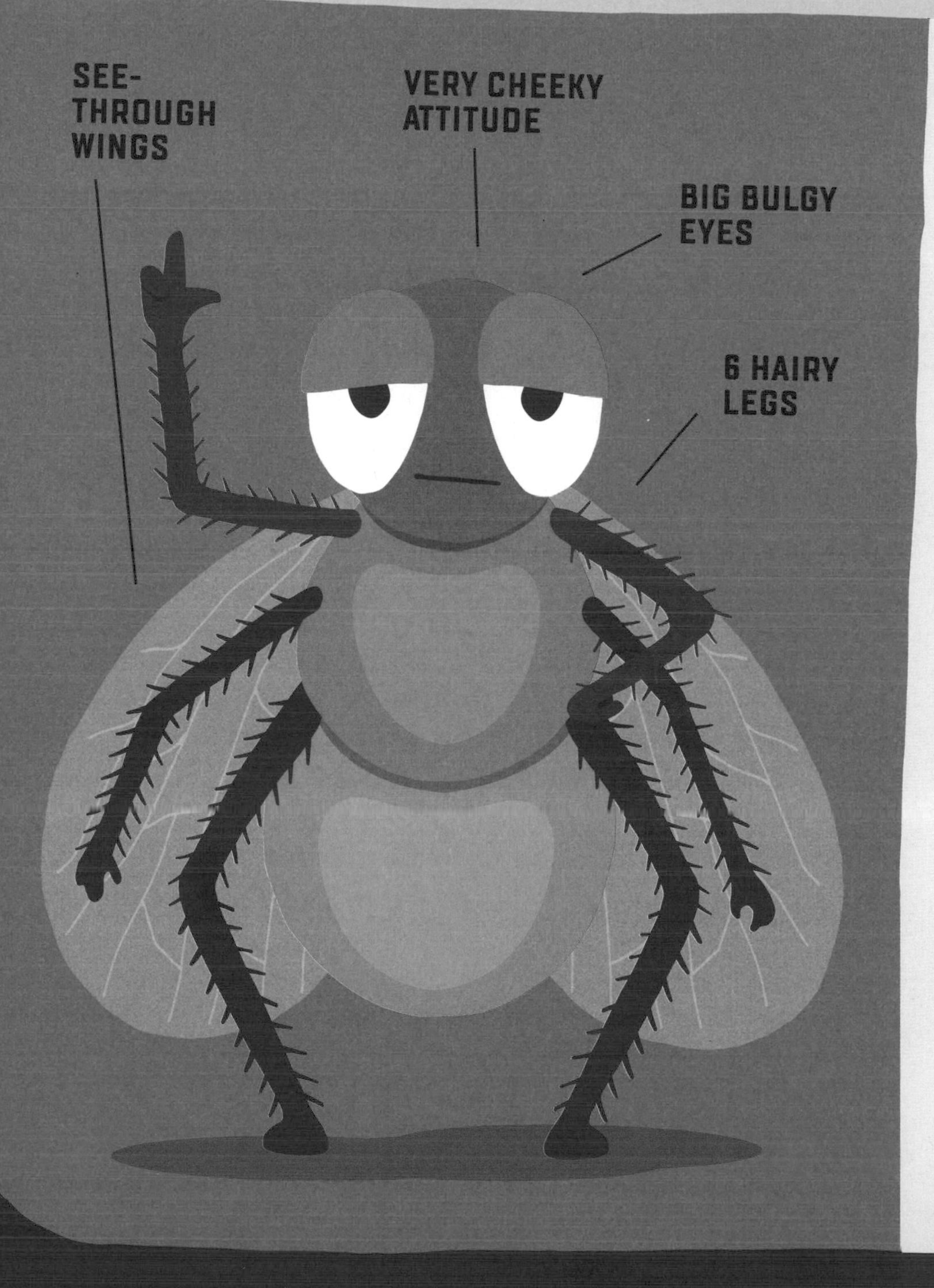

FACT FILE:

- LOVES SWEET TREATS, ESPECIALLY CAKE!
- ALSO LIKES EATING RUBBISH AND OTHER STINKY STUFF. URGH!
- CARRIES QUITE A FEW GERMS AROUND WHICH YOU WOULDN'T WANT ON A BIRTHDAY CAKE. YUCK!
- DEFINITELY NOT INVITED TO THE PARTY!

Spyder quickly packed her spy-kit, and set off.

Just getting around the house was a near-impossible mission,

but that didn't bother Spyder.

DANGER* was her middle name!

*Actually, it's Dorothy!

Soon, she came face to face
with her first obstacle:
a huge, strange, hairy creature
with terrible breath.

*It's too **BIG** to be a fly!*
she thought.

Phew!

It was only
Douglas,
the family
pooch.

Sorry, my furry friend.
No time to chat.
I spy a naughty fly!

Bluebottle was heading
for the bathroom.

Spyder gave chase...

but she didn't notice a thudding
sound that was getting louder...

WATCH OUT!

Danger was afoot.

After the close shave with
Mr Webster's Sock of Doom,
Spyder decided she'd
be safer higher up.

There's that bothersome Bluebottle.

COOEE!

Spyder swung down...

but could
not see the
pesky pest
anywhere.
Until...

Bluebottle
zoomed
down...

and knocked poor
Spyder into the bath.

OUCH!

Spyder landed on her bottom with a THUMP! Bluebottle chuckled. He knew baths were the one place spiders had trouble getting out of.

Ha, ha!
Now I'm off to have my cake AND eat it!

"This fly is really starting to bug me!"
sighed Spyder.

Just then Spyder's phone beeped again.

FOR YOUR EYES ONLY!
Bluebottle is on his way to the kitchen... CAKE IN DANGER! You must hurry!

She looked around the tub for an escape route...

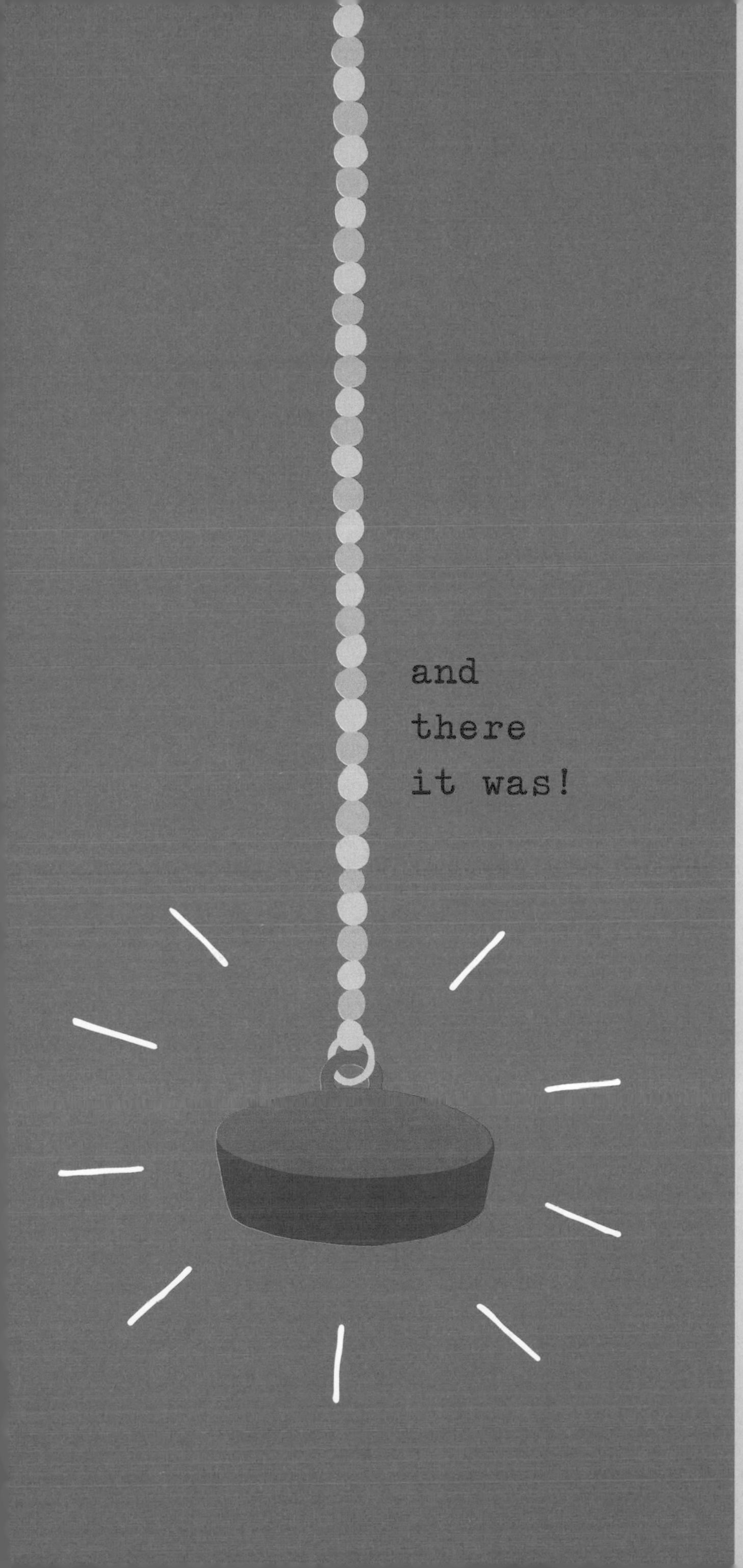

and
there
it was!

QUICK,
SPYDER!
There's
no
time
to
lose!

Safely out of the bathtub,
Spyder whizzed downstairs
as fast as she could.

I love my job!

In the kitchen,
Bluebottle was
circling hungrily.

Sugar

· TASTY ·
LEMONADE

Spyder would have to think on her feet
(lucky she had lots of them!).

Tom's cake looked splendid.
Bluebottle was sure to
spot it soon.

Spyder threw out a fine silk line...

...and bravely climbed across.

She spun a super strong web...

and then she waited...

YUM!
HAPPY BIRTHDAY
TO **ME!**

Bluebottle spied the cake
and dived down at top speed...

straight into Spyder's sticky web!

Boing!

Oh, bother!

Spyder had saved the day - and the cake!

She cleared away her web and soon the cake was as good as new.

MISSION ACCOMPLISHED!

Well done, Spyder! I'm sure the Websters will be very happy!

RING! RING!

MISS MONEY SPIDER

AAAA
A

RRGH!
SPIDER!

...or maybe not!

SPIDER FACTS WEBsite!

STRONG!

A spider's web may look thin and flimsy, but it is in fact very STRONG.

A spider's silk is even stronger than steel!

SCARY!

The fear of spiders is called...
ARACHNOPHOBIA
but spiders are actually a lot more scared of humans!

SPEEDY!

Some spiders are VERY fast indeed and could run even faster than a car if they were the same size as us!

SUPER-SIZE!

Spiders come in all shapes and sizes.

Some can even grow as BIG as this book!

TOP SECRET
1 2 3
4 5 6
7 8 9
0
THE EVENING SPIN
GOLIATH TARANTULA
& GIANT HUNTSMAN
BATTLE IT OUT FOR WORLD'S BIGGEST SPIDER
PASSPORT
CHOCO
0:08
I ♥ TEA
MI-8
SPYDER

Tee hee!
And I thought flies
had a hard time!